The Soccer Shoe Clue

"Eewww!" Amara Shane cried out. Her voice echoed off the metal lockers in the girls' locker room. "There's something yucky in my soccer shoe!"

"I can't see anything," Nancy Drew said. "You'll have to take off your shoe."

Amara wrinkled up her nose and made a face. But she took her shoe off. She used only two fingers of each hand, so she wouldn't have to touch it much.

All the girls in the room said, "Eewww! Gross!"

Amara's knee sock was covered with something slimy. Something dark red and slimy. . . .

THE

NANCY DREW
NOTEBOOKS®

The Soccer Shoe Clue

CAROLYN KEENE

ILLUSTRATED BY ANTHONY ACCARDO

SCHOLASTIC INC.

New York Toronto London Auckland Sydney
Mexico City New Delhi Hong Kong Buenos Aires

ISBN 0-439-41983-2

12 11 10 9 8 7 6 5 4   2 3 4 5 6 7/0

Printed in the U.S.A.   40

First Scholastic printing, September 2002

Cover art by Joanie Schwarz

The Soccer Shoe Clue

1

Team Tricks

Eewww. . . .Yuck!" Amara Shane cried out. Her voice echoed off the metal lockers in the girls' locker room.

"What's wrong?" eight-year-old Nancy Drew asked. She looked up as she finished putting on her shin guards.

"There's something yucky in my soccer shoe," Amara said. "Something sticky. It's gross!"

Nancy looked around for her friend George Fayne. George was the captain of the soccer team. She would help Amara. But George was not in the locker room.

All the other girls on the team watched as Nancy got up and walked over to Amara.

"Let me see," Nancy said.

Amara was sitting on a wooden bench in the locker room. School was out for the day. Now the third-grade girls' soccer team was getting ready for practice. Backpacks and jackets were scattered all over the place.

"I don't want to touch it," Amara said. She stuck out her foot to show Nancy.

"I can't see anything," Nancy said. "You'll have to take off your shoe."

Amara wrinkled up her nose and made a face. But she took her shoe off. She used only two fingers of each hand, so she wouldn't have to touch it much.

When she pulled her shoe off, all the girls in the room said, "Eewww! Gross!"

Amara's kneesock was covered with something slimy. Something dark red and slimy. Nancy bent down to take a closer look. It really was gross.

All the other girls crowded around Amara. All except Carrie Rodis. She kept putting on her own soccer shoes.

Carrie was new at Carl Sandburg Elementary School. She had just moved into Nancy's neighborhood. She had joined the Tigers team the week before.

"That's the third mean trick someone has played on us this week," Nancy said.

"I'll help you clean it up," Erin Kelly said to Amara.

Nancy smiled. Erin was just about the nicest person in the whole school.

"Thanks," Amara said.

"Girls? Are you ready to practice?"

Nancy turned around. Coach Santos was standing in the doorway. She was Julia Santos's mother.

Both Julia and her mother were very good soccer players. They were from Brazil, and soccer was a big sport there.

"We're not quite ready," Nancy told Coach Santos. "Someone put something icky in Amara's shoe."

"Oh, no! Not another prank," Coach Santos said.

"I can't play goalie with my shoe all slimy," Amara complained.

"Well, clean it up," Coach Santos said. She smiled at Amara. "Put on a clean sock, too. And, everyone else, hurry up. It looks as if it's going to rain. Let's get practice started."

Nancy quickly pulled on her soccer cleats. She checked the elastic on her reddish blond ponytail. It was still tight. Then she glanced around the locker room.

Hey, Nancy thought. Where *is* George? Nancy wanted to go look for her friend. But Coach Santos was watching her.

"Come on, Tigers. The sky is getting cloudier all the time," Coach Santos urged. "Let's get outside while we still can play."

Nancy pulled a red sweatshirt on over her T-shirt. Then she grabbed her soccer ball and a net bag with two other balls. She hurried to follow the other girls outside.

"This is creepy," Lindsay Mitchell whispered to Nancy as they walked toward the field. "On Wednesday someone tied big knots in the laces of my soccer shoes."

"I know," Nancy said with a nod. "Someone let the air out of Julia's ball on Friday, too."

"You're a detective," Lindsay said. "Maybe you can figure out who's doing this—and who put the icky stuff in Amara's shoe."

Maybe I can, Nancy thought. At least I can try.

She saw Carrie Rodis walking ahead of them all by herself. Nancy had noticed that Carrie had ignored Amara. She hadn't seemed to care about the goo in Amara's shoe. Was Carrie the one trying to hurt the team?

There was no way to know for sure. But *someone* had been playing tricks on the soccer team. And Carrie had a good reason to do it.

Before she had moved, Carrie had played for the Lions. They were another elementary school team. And they were the Tigers' biggest rivals!

Maybe Carrie still wants the Lions to

beat us, Nancy thought. Maybe she's trying to make our team look bad so that her old friends will win.

"Hey, Nancy! Lindsay!" a voice called.

Nancy and Lindsay turned around and saw George running toward them. Her dark curls bounced as she ran. Her long legs carried her quickly across the field.

"Where were you?" Nancy asked.

"I couldn't find my shin guards," George answered. "I thought maybe I left them in my cubby, so I went back to see. But they weren't there. Finally I found them in the trash."

"You're kidding!" Lindsay said.

George shook her head. "Someone must have taken them out of my backpack."

"Something else happened in the locker room today," Lindsay said quickly. She loved to be the first one to tell stories.

"What are you talking about?" George asked.

6

Lindsay told George about the yucky stuff in Amara's shoe. George frowned. She looked down at her shin guards. "I think it was Carrie."

Nancy was surprised that George suspected Carrie, too. She didn't want to say that in front of Lindsay, though, so she said, "But she's a good player."

"Who cares?" George said. "She acts like she's the only one who's any good. She's always telling me how to pass the ball. Like I don't already know."

The three girls started walking toward the field again.

Nancy squinted. Carrie was kicking a soccer ball. It flew into the air and went into the goal. It was a good shot. It would have been hard for a goalie to catch it.

"She's one of our best players," Lindsay said.

George made a face. "So what," she said.

Just then a cheer went up from the sidelines. Nancy looked across the field.

Two girls were standing there. They were watching the team play.

The ball rolled toward Carrie, and she kicked it again. Again it sailed into the goal.

"Way to go, Carrie!" the girls on the sidelines yelled.

"Who are they?" Nancy asked. "I don't recognize them."

"I do," George said in a grouchy voice.

"Well? Are you going to tell me?" Nancy asked.

"That's Margot Bachwood and Tonya Morris," George said. "I remember them from last year's games. They're two of the best soccer players on the Lions team. And the Lions are our team's worst enemies!"

2

Soccer Spies

What are those Lions doing here?" Nancy asked. She stared across the field at Margot and Tonya.

"I don't know," George said.

"*I* know," Lindsay said.

Nancy shook her head and laughed. Lindsay always knew everything— because she always eavesdropped on other people's conversations.

"So why are they here?" Nancy asked.

"I heard Carrie telling someone at lunch," Lindsay explained. "Her best friends are picking her up after soccer practice today. They're having a sleep-over at Margot's house tonight."

"Oh, great," George said. "She's

probably going to tell them all our soccer plays."

"Girls! Let's go!" Coach Santos called to them from the middle of the field. "I want to talk to you—now!"

All the girls gathered around their coach.

"Girls, I'm very unhappy about what happened to Amara's shoe today," Coach Santos began. "These pranks have got to stop. To be a good soccer player, you have to work hard on your skills. And you can't work hard if you're busy playing pranks on one another. Do you understand?"

The girls nodded.

"All right," Coach Santos said. "Then let's line up. We need to work on kicking now."

Nancy, George, and Lindsay hurried to get in line. They lined up facing the goal.

Amara had pinned her hair in a bun so it wouldn't get in her eyes when she tried to catch the ball. Amara played goalie. As each girl kicked the ball,

Amara tried to keep it from going past her into the net.

Melissa Adams was first in line. She was short, with red hair and dimples.

"Melissa's not a very good player," George whispered. "She needs a *lot* of practice."

Nancy and George watched Melissa. She took a long time to kick the ball. When she finally did kick it, her foot slipped. She fell. The ball barely rolled across the grass. It didn't even go near the goal.

Nancy heard Carrie's friends laughing.

"That's not nice," George whispered to Nancy. "Even though she *is* a lousy player."

Nancy nodded, then glared at the girls. Who did they think they were, anyway?

Carrie was next in line. She kicked the ball so hard, it zoomed into the net right past Amara's fingertips.

"Yay, Carrie!" the two girls on the sidelines cheered.

Carrie waved at them. Then she ran

around to the back of the line, where Nancy and George were standing.

"Nice shot!" Coach Santos called to Carrie. "Keep up the good work!"

George and Nancy looked at each other and rolled their eyes.

"No wonder she's so stuck-up," George whispered. "Coach Santos loves her. And she even has her own cheerleaders right over there."

Carrie tapped George on the arm. "Hey, George," she said. "If you use the top of your shoe when you kick, instead of your toe, the ball goes farther."

"Yeah, right. And if you use a rocket launcher, I'll bet it really flies," George answered.

Carrie looked hurt, but Nancy laughed at the joke. Then she leaned closer to George, so that Carrie wouldn't hear.

"Is she right?" Nancy whispered. "Is that the way to kick the ball really far?"

George nodded. "Yes. Coach Santos showed us last year. I'll show you later—when *she's* not around."

"Thanks," Nancy said with a smile.

Nancy wanted to learn as much as she could about soccer. Most of the other girls on the team had played before. This was Nancy's first season. She had just joined the team that spring.

A minute later it was Nancy's turn to kick. She ran up and kicked the ball the way Carrie had said—with the top of her shoe. The ball sailed straight for the goal. But Amara caught it.

"Nice try," Coach Santos called. "But next time try not to kick it right to the goalie."

Nancy looked over at Carrie's friends from her old school. They were looking at her and giggling.

For the rest of the soccer practice, Carrie's friends watched Nancy and the other Tigers. They giggled and pointed at them when they made mistakes. Nancy couldn't wait for the practice to be over.

Finally it was time to go back into the locker room and change.

"Wait for me!" George called as Nancy ran toward the school.

"Hurry!" Nancy called.

"Why?" George asked.

Nancy didn't answer. She just ran into the locker room and went straight to her backpack. She took out her special blue notebook. It was the one she used when she was trying to solve a mystery.

Nancy sat down on the floor and crossed her legs. She opened her notebook to the first clean page. Then she took out her favorite new pen. It had purple ink.

At the top of the page Nancy wrote, "The Soccer Mystery."

Then she wrote:

Suspects:
Carrie Rodis
Margot Bachwood
Tonya Morris

Then Nancy looked around the room. All the other girls were coming in. They took off their shin guards and soccer cleats, and put on their regular shoes.

Nancy just sat on the floor and

watched them for a while. Who else could have done it? Nancy wondered.

The answer was easy—almost anyone!

"What are you doing, Nancy?" Melissa Adams asked. "You're just staring at us."

"She's trying to solve the mystery," George said. "Shhh. Don't talk to her. She's probably thinking really hard."

Nancy gave George a small smile. George was right. Nancy *was* thinking hard.

Finally most of the girls finished changing their shoes and left.

Julia Santos was waiting for her mother. Coach Santos was in the office next to the gym. Nancy stood up and looked around. "Hey, where are *my* sneakers?" she asked.

"On the floor where you left them?" George asked.

"No," Nancy said. She shook her head. "They're gone!"

3

Missing Shoes and Enemy Clues

That's terrible!" Julia said. "I can't believe someone would steal your shoes."

"Me, either," Nancy said. "It's so mean."

Nancy felt her face growing hot. All these pranks were taking the fun out of being on the soccer team.

But then Nancy remembered what her father always said to do when she was trying to solve a puzzle or a mystery: "Stay cool. Think clearly. And don't jump to conclusions."

That meant, Don't make up your mind until you know the facts.

"Maybe they're not stolen," Nancy said. "Let's look around."

Nancy, George, and Julia began to search the locker room. Nancy looked under the wooden benches. She looked on top of the lockers. She opened all the empty lockers.

Then she looked behind a metal cabinet that was at the end of the room.

"Hey, look what I found!" Nancy cried.

George came running over. Julia had gone to the office to tell her mother about the missing sneakers. "What?"

"An empty jar of red currant jelly," Nancy announced as she held it up.

"What's red currant jelly?" George asked.

"It's made from red berries, called currants," Nancy explained. "I had it once in a restaurant."

"What is red currant jelly doing here? That's weird," George said.

"I think I know," Nancy said. "It's

icky. And slimy. And red. I think this is what someone put in Amara's shoe."

"You're so smart," George said, smiling at her friend.

Nancy put the jar back where she had found it. Then she walked over to her notebook. She picked up her purple pen and wrote, "Clue #1: Red currant jelly in Amara's shoe."

"Who do you think put it there?" George asked.

"I don't know," Nancy said. "But it's definitely a clue. So don't tell anyone."

"Okay," George said. "But we still haven't found your sneakers. And I've looked everywhere."

"I know," Nancy said. "I guess I'll have to walk home in my soccer cleats—or my socks."

Nancy put her hands on her hips and let out an angry sigh. "How could someone on my own team steal my shoes?" she asked George.

"I know how you feel," George said. She put her arm around Nancy's shoulder.

Then George bent over and picked up her backpack. "Oh, no!" George shouted.

There on the floor, under George's backpack, were Nancy's shoes!

Nancy and George burst out laughing.

Just then Coach Santos and Julia came back into the room. "What's this about missing sneakers?" the coach asked.

"I must have put my backpack on top of them," George said. "I didn't even notice." She handed them to Nancy.

"You're the thief!" Nancy yelled. She laughed as she put the sneakers on.

Still giggling, Nancy grabbed her notebook. She picked up her purple pen and started to write.

"What are you writing?" George asked.

Nancy gave George a teasing smile. When she finished, she turned the notebook around so George could see.

It said, "Note to Nancy: Remember— when shoes are missing, the number one suspect is George Fayne!"

George laughed and helped Nancy pack up her soccer gear. They waved at Coach Santos and Julia as they left. Then the two girls walked to Nancy's house.

Nancy lived in a big house on a tree-lined street. Her house was only a few blocks away from school. When she and George got there, Hannah Gruen had a snack waiting for them.

Hannah was the housekeeper. She had lived with the Drew family ever since Nancy was three years old. That's when Nancy's mother had died.

Now Hannah was like a mother to Nancy. She gave Nancy a hug when she came in the door.

"Mmmmm! Blueberry muffins!" George cried out as she dropped her things on one of the kitchen chairs.

"Don't eat too many," Hannah said to George. "Your cousin is coming over. Save some for her."

"Bess?" Nancy said, sounding happy.

Hannah nodded. "Your father made plans with Bess's and George's parents.

Since it's Friday night, he's taking all three of you girls to the mall. For dinner and a movie."

"Yay!" Nancy and George both said at once.

Twenty minutes later Bess Marvin arrived. With straight blond hair pulled back in a ponytail and a round face, Bess looked nothing like George. But she was George's cousin and Nancy's other best friend. The three of them always did everything together.

While Bess ate two blueberry muffins, Nancy told her about the soccer pranks.

"It sounds like Carrie Rodis did it," Bess announced when Nancy finished talking. "I'll bet she's really jealous of George. I wouldn't trust her if I were you."

"Well, I'm not sure," Nancy said. "I'm going to wait and see."

For the next hour the girls played in Nancy's room. Then Carson Drew came home. He took them to the mall for dinner. Then they all walked around the mall, waiting for the movie to start.

"Hey, look who's here," Nancy said.

She pointed to three girls and two grown-ups. They were looking in a store window.

"It's Carrie," Bess said. "But who is she with?"

"Her friends from her old school," Nancy answered. "Margot and Tonya."

"She still hangs out with them all the time," George complained. "And look. Carrie is wearing purple and white— *their* school colors."

Nancy turned to her father. "Daddy, can we go look in that store window?"

Carson Drew nodded. "But don't go anywhere else. I'll be waiting for you right here, where I can see you. On this bench."

Nancy, Bess, and George hurried over to the store window. It was filled with storybook toys and books about fairy-tale characters.

Margot, Tonya, and Carrie were looking at a comb and mirror set that had a picture of Snow White on it. They didn't see Nancy coming up behind them.

"Mirror, mirror, on the wall," Bess said loudly to Nancy. "Who's the fairest of *them* all?"

Carrie and her friends jumped. They spun around quickly.

"Oh, hi!" Carrie said, sounding surprised.

"Hi," Nancy said.

"Hi," Bess said.

"Are you getting ready for our soccer game tomorrow?" George asked, staring at Carrie.

Carrie frowned. "What do you mean? I'm just shopping."

"Well, do you think you should be shopping with our team's enemies?" George said.

"That's not fair!" Carrie said angrily. "These are my friends."

"I know," George said. "That's what I mean."

Carrie looked upset. "I don't see

what's wrong with being with my friends," she said.

"That depends on what you're telling them about our team," George said.

"Come on," Nancy said, grabbing George by the arm. "Let's go."

She took Bess's arm, too, and started to pull her friends away. But Tonya called after them.

"I hear your team is jinxed," she called. "I hear bad things happen all the time."

George turned around and glared angrily at Carrie.

"I guess you tell your *friends* everything," she snapped. "I guess you've told them all our plays, too!"

"I did not!" Carrie said.

"I don't care," George said. "It won't matter when we play the Bluejays tomorrow. We'll still win. And we'll win when we play *your* team next week, too."

"Really?" Tonya said. "Even if your goalie has goo in her shoes?"

Carrie and her friends started giggling again.

"What do you know about that?" George demanded.

"All I know is, I'm glad I'm not on the Tigers team," Tonya said. "In fact, I'd be careful tomorrow, if I were you."

"What's that supposed to mean?" George asked.

"It's just that everyone is saying . . ." Tonya said.

"What?" Nancy asked.

Tonya gave Nancy a mean smile. "That being a Tiger is bad luck!"

4

Bad Luck Tigers

Go, George! Get in there! Steal the ball! Run!" a man shouted from the sidelines.

Nancy knew the voice. It was Melissa Adams's father. He came to every game. He always shouted a lot.

It was early in the first half of the Saturday morning game against the Bluejays. Already the Tigers were losing. The score was 1–0.

"Go, George! Run! We've got to score!" Mr. Adams screamed at the top of his lungs.

George dribbled the ball with her feet until she was close to the Bluejays' goal. But all nine Bluejays were bunched up in front of her. She couldn't get a good shot.

"Pass! Pass it, George!" Mr. Adams screamed.

"Go, Tigers!" another parent on the sidelines yelled. "Yay, team!"

Nancy looked around. There was no one to pass it to, except Carrie. George saw that Carrie was free, too. But instead of passing the ball, George kicked it toward the goal.

The ball went straight to one of the Bluejays' players. The player headed the ball. That is what it was called when you hit the ball with your head. Nancy had just learned how to do it. It sort of hurt, but it was fun, too.

"Keep trying!" one of the parents shouted.

"George! You should have passed!" Mr. Adams yelled. "Next time pass the ball! Now come on, Tigers. Let's go! We've got to win!"

Nancy didn't run up to the Bluejays' goal. She was a fullback. That meant she was supposed to stay in the back part of the field. She was part of the defense.

"Come on, Nancy, get in there!" Mr. Adams yelled.

Boy, I'm glad he's not my father, Nancy thought. Mr. Adams yelled at everyone all the time.

And Melissa wasn't even playing just then! She was sitting on the sidelines, waiting her turn.

For the next ten minutes the Tigers tried hard to score a goal. The parents cheered and screamed. But when the whistle blew, the score was still Bluejays 1–Tigers 0.

Nancy ran to the sidelines, panting and thirsty. All the players were hot and thirsty, even though it was a cool spring day. The Tigers gathered around the big water cooler that George's mother had brought to the game.

"Good job, Tigers," Coach Santos said. "You held them to only one goal. Have a drink and then I'll tell you who's playing next half."

Nancy grabbed two cups and gave

one to George. They waited for their turn at the water cooler. Lindsay Mitchell was first.

She filled her paper cup and then took a huge gulp.

Suddenly she spit out the whole mouthful, all over the grass. Some of it dripped on her blue-and-orange soccer uniform.

"Oh, yuck!" Lindsay said. "It's salt water!"

"Blechhh!" Erin said. She had just taken a drink, too.

"What's wrong?" Coach Santos asked.

"George's mom brought salt water," Lindsay said.

"No, she did not!" George said.

"Well, someone *put* salt in it," Lindsay said.

"Not another prank!" Coach Santos cried. "Okay, George. Where is your mother right now?"

"She had to go somewhere," George said. "She dropped me off with the

cooler and then left. She'll be back when the game is over."

Coach Santos picked up the cooler. "I'll ask another parent to go get us some fresh water," she said. "Let's not panic."

Nancy wasn't panicking. But she was really thirsty. She didn't want to play another half without a drink.

"I have a box of juice in my backpack," Erin Kelly said. "I'll get it. Maybe we can all share."

"That's nice of you," Coach Santos said. "But I don't think one box of juice is enough for fourteen girls. You drink it, and we'll wait for the water."

"Can I play next half?" Melissa Adams asked. "I'm not thirsty or tired at all."

"Not yet, Melissa," Coach Santos said.

Nancy pulled George aside.

"Look," Nancy said. She pointed at Carrie, who was pulling something from her backpack. "Carrie has her own water bottle. She doesn't even care about what happened."

"Do you think she was the one who put salt in the water?" George asked.

"I don't know. Erin has her own drink, too. So they are both suspects," Nancy said. "But I don't think Erin would do something like this. She's too nice."

"I think Carrie did it," George said.

George walked up to Carrie and stared her right in the face. "How come you just happened to bring your own water bottle?" George asked.

"I always bring my own," Carrie said in a snooty voice. "That's what they taught us to do on the Lions team. The *best* players always do."

Nancy and George didn't know what to say. They turned and walked away. Nancy was still thirsty. And being thirsty made her really angry at who-ever had played this trick on the team.

Finally Amara's father returned with a cooler of fresh water. Nancy and George ran over to get a drink.

Then Nancy looked around at the crowd of parents and kids who were watching the game. Were Carrie's friends at the game, too? There were so many people, Nancy couldn't tell.

Soon it was time to start the second half.

For the rest of the game the Tigers played hard. Carrie scored one goal and tied up the game. But after that no one scored. Not even George!

"I guess you *are* the Bad Luck Tigers," Carrie said as she and Nancy came off the field.

"What do you mean 'you'? You're a Tiger, too," Nancy said. "Remember?"

"Oh, yeah?" Carrie said angrily. "Well, I sure don't feel like one!"

5

In the News

Nancy woke up early Wednesday morning. She climbed out of bed and sat at her desk in her nightgown. She stared at her special blue notebook.

"Hey, there, Pudding Pie," Nancy's father said. He was standing in the doorway to her room.

Nancy smiled. She liked it when her father called her Pudding Pie. It was his special nickname for her.

"Hi, Daddy," Nancy said.

Carson Drew came into the room.

"Why aren't you getting ready for school?" he asked.

"Because I've decided," Nancy said. "I'm not getting dressed until I solve the soccer mystery."

Carson Drew laughed. "What's the problem?" he asked.

Nancy pointed to her list of suspects. "I have three suspects," she said. "But I don't know if any of them did it."

She held up the notebook so he could see the three names: Carrie, Margot, and Tonya.

"Do you have any clues?" her father asked.

"Just a jar of red currant jelly," Nancy said.

Carson laughed. "How about witnesses?" he asked. "Did anyone see anything?"

"Nope," Nancy said.

"Hmmm," Carson said. "I see the problem."

"So what should I do?" Nancy asked.

"Well," Carson said, "maybe it would help to figure out who *didn't* do it."

"You mean, make a list of people who *aren't* suspects?" Nancy said. "That's a great idea! Thanks, Daddy."

Right away Nancy thought of a few people who couldn't be guilty. People like Julia Santos. She was the coach's daughter. She would never play tricks on the soccer team.

There were others, too. But Nancy didn't have time to make the list just then. She had to get dressed. She was almost late for school!

Quickly she put on sweatpants and a sweater. She packed up her books and soccer gear and hurried downstairs. She ate some cereal and drank a glass of juice. Then she ran most of the way to school.

When she got there, all the girls were huddled together in a circle. It looked as if they were reading something— but what?

"What's going on?" Nancy asked as she ran up to join them.

"Nancy, look at this," George said. She held up a piece of paper in front of Nancy so Nancy could read it.

It was a homemade newspaper, written by Brenda Carlton, another third grader. Brenda made copies on her

computer at home and brought them to school.

Nancy wrinkled her nose. She didn't like Brenda very much. Brenda didn't like Nancy, either.

The newspaper story read:

TIGERS LOSE WHEN CAPTAIN BRINGS SALT WATER TO SOCCER GAME

The soccer game between the Tigers and the Bluejays on Saturday was a big mess. None of the Tigers played very well after the first half. Could it be because the water cooler was filled with salt water?

Yes, it's true! George Fayne, captain of the team, brought a whole cooler full of salt water to the game!

Of course the team lost. Who can play soccer when they are so thirsty?

Many pranks and tricks have been happening to the team lately. Last week Amara Shane found a whole jar of red currant jelly in her soccer shoe!

The big question is: Who is doing this? And why isn't the captain doing anything?

If the Tigers are going to win, they'll need a captain who can really be a leader.

Nancy's mouth fell open as she read the story.

"I don't believe this!" she said to George. "The Tigers didn't lose. We tied."

"I know," George said angrily.

"And how can she blame you for the salt water?" Nancy went on. "She doesn't know what happened. She wasn't even at the game!"

"Yes, she was," Julia Santos said.

"She was?" Nancy asked.

Julia nodded. Lindsay Mitchell nodded, too.

"I saw Brenda on Saturday," Lindsay said. "She was hanging around at the soccer field."

"Really?" Nancy said. "But she doesn't even like soccer."

Lindsay started to say something else. But just then the bell rang. It was time to go into school.

All the girls hurried into the classroom. Nancy led the way. She was looking for Brenda.

Nancy found her sitting at her desk, writing something on a piece of notebook paper. Brenda put her hand over the paper the minute she saw Nancy.

"Oh, hi," Brenda said. She gave Nancy a phony smile.

"Brenda," Nancy said. "I just saw your newspaper. And I have a question. How did you know about the jelly in Amara's shoe?"

"Everyone knows about the goo in Amara's shoe," Brenda answered.

"But no one knew it was jelly," Nancy said.

For a moment Brenda looked surprised. She reached up and tugged on a strand of her dark brown hair. She frowned. Then she said, "I have ways to find things out."

"Like what?" Nancy asked.

"I'm not telling," Brenda said. "And you can't make me." Then she smiled again. It was a sneaky smile this time. "All I'll say is this. I'm getting my information from a really good source."

"Who?" Nancy asked again.

"Someone on your team!"

6

Doodles
and Clues

What a mess," Nancy said as she stared at her special blue notebook. She reached into a nearby bowl of popcorn and took a big buttery piece. Then she popped it into her mouth.

"Why is your notebook such a mess?" Bess asked. She was sprawled across the end of Nancy's bed. From there she could reach the popcorn more easily.

George sat cross-legged on the floor by Nancy's bed.

It was Friday night. Bess and George were sleeping over at Nancy's house. Saturday was the big game against the Lions.

"Because I scribbled all over the page," Nancy said. "I was trying to solve this mystery yesterday at lunch. And I was talking to Lindsay at the same time."

"Big mistake," George said with a laugh.

Nancy nodded. "I accidentally wrote down half the things she was telling me. Gossip and stuff."

Bess took the notebook from Nancy and looked at it. "You're right," she said. "This is a mess. Listen to this list of names. Carrie, Margot Bachwood, Tonya Morris, Amara, Lindsay Mitchell, Melissa Adams, Julia Santos, George . . ."

Bess went on reading the names, and Nancy and George started giggling. It was true. Nancy had written down the name of almost every person on the soccer team!

"But I had a reason for that," Nancy said. "First I was making a list of suspects. Then I decided to make a list of all the

46

people who *aren't* suspects. I thought it would help me see who was left."

"Okay," Bess said. "But here it says, 'Melissa Adams's mom had a baby.' What does that have to do with soccer?"

Nancy giggled.

"And here it says, 'When shoes are missing, the number one suspect is George Fayne!'" Bess said.

George rolled over on the floor, laughing harder.

"What's so funny?" Bess asked. "Why is George a suspect? Do you really think she stole someone's shoes?"

"I know she did!" Nancy said, laughing.

"I don't get it," Bess said.

"It was really funny," George said. She explained to Bess about how Nancy's shoes had "disappeared."

"Give me the notebook," Nancy said. "I'm going to start over."

Nancy thought about all the pranks that had happened. She tried to remember who had been there each time.

Then she made a new list of all the

girls on the team. She crossed off the ones who had been the victims of pranks. People wouldn't play tricks on themselves, Nancy decided.

She also crossed off the ones who were absent on the days when the pranks happened.

When she was done, only three names were left:

Carrie Rodis
Erin Kelly
Melissa Adams

Nancy added one more name to the list: Brenda Carlton.

Then she showed the list to Bess and George.

"Why aren't Carrie's old friends on the list?" Bess asked.

"Because they weren't around when the trouble first started happening," Nancy explained. "And anyway, I don't think they could do it."

"Do what?" George asked.

"Sneak into the locker room at

school and put jelly in Amara's shoe," Nancy said. "They don't know their way around our school. How would they find out where to go?"

"You're right," George said. "But I don't know about Erin Kelly. She's too nice. She wouldn't do these mean things."

"I don't think so, either," Nancy said. "But she was there every time. And none of the pranks were ever done to her. So she's a suspect."

"What about Brenda Carlton?" Bess asked. "She's not even on the team. Do you really think she's a suspect?"

"She's so sneaky," Nancy said. "I can't be sure."

"Well, you've got to figure it out to-night," George said. "We have a game tomorrow."

"I can't," Nancy said. "I don't have enough clues."

Nancy felt bad. She didn't want to let the team down.

"So what are we going to do?" George said. "We're playing the Lions tomorrow. I don't want anything to go wrong."

"When we go to the game," Nancy said, "we can keep our eyes open. If someone tries to pull something, we'll see it."

When Nancy, George, and Bess got to the soccer field the next day, it was crowded. Two teams of older players were on the field, playing a game. It wasn't the Tigers' turn yet.

"The Tigers are warming up on the sidelines," Erin's father called to Nancy and George.

"Warming up is right," George called back. "It's freezing out here!"

Nancy shivered. The sky was cloudy. A cold April breeze blew through the trees. Nancy was glad she had worn a turtleneck shirt under her blue-and-orange soccer shirt.

She looked around and saw that lots of other girls had done the same thing. Melissa Adams had even worn red wool gloves. And blue jeans! She had them on *under* her soccer shorts. The outfit looked funny, but Nancy wished that she had worn long pants, too.

Nancy blew on her hands, trying to warm them.

"Do you see Carrie anywhere?" Nancy asked.

"Nope," George said. "I've been looking."

"George! Nancy! Let's go!" a man's voice called.

Nancy saw it was Melissa Adams's father. He picked up a soccer ball and threw it hard at George.

"You two need to start practicing!" he yelled. "You're late."

George rolled her eyes.

"He's not the coach," she said under her breath to Nancy.

George and Nancy waved to Lindsay Mitchell. They went over and found an empty spot near her. Then they started passing the ball back and forth to one another.

Nearby, Coach Santos was giving

Erin and Julia tips on how to dribble the ball better.

Finally Coach Santos called the team together.

"You girls look good today," Coach Santos said. "If you all play hard and stay in your positions, we can win."

Then she read their names from a paper on her clipboard. She told each girl what position she would play.

Carrie and George were both forwards. That meant they would be up front, trying to score.

Erin and Lindsay were two of the halfbacks. That meant they were in the middle. They helped the forwards *and* the fullbacks.

Nancy was playing fullback again. Amara was goalie. But three girls were not playing in the first half. Melissa Adams was one of them.

Melissa frowned. "No fair," she said. "I wanted to play."

"Everyone will get to play," Coach Santos said. "All right, team. Just remember the rules. Play hard. Play fair. And let's play a good game!"

Amara jumped up and ran over to the pile of soccer equipment. She picked up the special white shirt that the goalie always wore. She pulled it on over her head.

"Blecchhhh!" Amara yelled as she stuck her head out through the neck opening.

Nancy and the other girls looked up. Amara had white powder all over her hair and face. Even her brown arms had white powder freckles!

"Someone put powder inside this shirt!" Amara cried as she pulled it off again. White powder flew everywhere.

Nancy and George ran over to Amara.

"It smells like baby powder," Nancy said softly to George.

Coach Santos put her hands on her hips. She shook her head. "This is ridiculous!" she said.

Coach Santos hurried over to help Amara. She took the goalie's shirt and shook it until most of the baby powder was gone. Then she handed it back to Amara.

"Here," she said. "Hurry up and put it on. The Lions are already on the field, waiting for us. We have to start the game soon."

"I can't!" Amara cried.

"Why not?" Coach Santos asked. "What's wrong now?"

"My lucky goalie gloves! They were here just a minute ago. Now they're gone!"

7

Notebook Snoop

Does anyone else have a pair of gloves that Amara can use?" Coach Santos asked the team.

Nancy looked around. All the girls were shaking their heads no.

"Not just any gloves," Amara said. "I have to have my *lucky* gloves. With the rubber pads on the fingers. They help me catch the ball. I need them for good luck!"

"Where did you put them?" Coach Santos asked.

"Right here, near the water cooler and soccer balls," Amara said.

"Okay, everyone," Coach Santos said. "Start looking for the gloves. But we've got to hurry. The Lions are ready to play. And the referee just gave me a signal. We have to be on the field in five minutes, or else we lose the game."

All the girls started searching for Amara's gloves. Nancy wanted to help, too. But she had something else on her mind. Something more important.

Another pair of gloves!

Nancy was almost certain she had just seen Melissa Adams wearing a pair of red woolen gloves. She closed her eyes and tried to picture it.

Yes! Melissa was wearing gloves, but there was something odd about them. They looked really thick. Maybe she was hiding something inside them.

All of a sudden Nancy remembered something else. Something she had written in her notebook, on the page with the scribbles.

She hurried to the place on the sidelines where she had left her backpack. Her notebook was in it.

But someone was already standing

there. Wait a minute, Nancy thought. What's *she* doing here?

The girl's back was turned, but Nancy could tell that it was Brenda Carlton. She was reading Nancy's notebook!

"What are you doing?" Nancy asked sharply.

Brenda jumped and spun around. "Oh!" she said. "You scared me."

"Good," Nancy said. "Now—what are you doing with my notebook?"

"Uh . . . I was just trying to help you solve this mystery," Brenda said. "I thought maybe I could figure out who's been playing all these tricks."

"No, you weren't," Nancy said. "You were spying and snooping. Trying to find out things so you could write about them in your newspaper. You've probably done it before, too. That's how you found out about the jelly in Amara's shoe."

Brenda smiled. "Well, I told you I had a good source," she said with a mean little laugh.

Nancy held out her hand. "Give me my notebook back," she said.

With a shrug Brenda handed it over. Then she turned and started to leave.

"Wait a minute," Nancy said. "Why have you been coming to our games? You don't play soccer. You're not on the team."

"My brother plays for the sixth-grade team," Brenda said. "They play just before you. Not that it's any of your business."

Then she tossed her hair over her shoulders and walked away.

I'll have to be very careful with my notebook from now on, Nancy decided.

But just then she had something important to do. She opened her notebook and looked at the page that was scribbled on.

In the margin there was a doodle. It said, "Melissa Adams's mom had a baby."

"That's what I thought," Nancy said softly. "Baby powder!"

Then she looked around. Her eyes scanned the crowd, looking for Melissa.

Finally she saw her. Melissa was running back from the parking lot.

What's she doing over there? Nancy wondered.

Nancy glanced back at the field. There wasn't much time left. The Lions were standing in their positions, just waiting for the Tigers. And the referee was looking at his watch. If the Tigers didn't get on the field soon, they would lose.

As fast as she could, Nancy ran toward the parking lot.

There must be something there, Nancy thought. Some kind of clue.

Otherwise, what was Melissa doing?

8

Caught
Red-Handed

Nancy followed the path Melissa had taken through the parking lot.

She checked the ground.

She looked between cars.

Finally she looked in the big metal trash can. It was at the end of the last row of cars.

Amara's lucky gloves were right on top—in the trash!

Nancy grabbed the gloves and ran back toward the field.

"Amara! I've got them!" she called, waving the gloves in the air.

"Thank goodness!" Coach Santos cried out. "Just in time. All right, girls. Let's get onto the field."

"Come on!" Mr. Adams yelled. "Let's win!"

Nancy knew she had to hurry onto the field. But first she ran up to Melissa, who was standing off to one side.

"I know what you did," Nancy said.

"What?" Melissa snapped. Then she quickly added. "Don't tell anyone— please!"

"I can't talk now," Nancy said. "Wait until the half is over."

Nancy ran onto the field. The referee hadn't blown the whistle yet to start the game. So Nancy motioned to George, who was standing in the center of the field near the ball.

"I found out who's been doing all this," Nancy said quickly when George came over. "And it isn't Carrie. I think we've been unfair to her."

"Really?" George said. "Who is it?"

"Tell you later!" Nancy called, running to her own position.

For the first ten minutes of the game, no one scored. The Lions were tough.

Their defense kept the Tigers from getting near the goal.

"Get in there! Let's go!" Mr. Adams yelled from the sidelines. "Pass the ball! Pass!"

We're doing our best, Nancy thought. She wished Mr. Adams would just cheer like the other parents.

Besides, George and Carrie were playing well together. Nancy saw George pass the ball to Carrie four times. Carrie looked happy. She smiled at George for the first time since she'd joined the team.

Then, near the end of the half, the Tigers got the ball. Carrie dribbled down the field toward the goal. But she couldn't get a good shot. She looked around and saw that no fullbacks from the Lions team were near George.

With a swift sideways kick, Carrie passed the ball to George. George trapped it with her shoe. Then she kicked it hard. The Lions goalie jumped for the ball. She missed.

George scored!

A minute later the referee blew the whistle. The half was over.

"Nice teamwork," Coach Santos said as George and Carrie came off the field. She told the team who would be playing in the second half. Then she said, "Everyone rest and drink some water."

Nancy gave George a pat on the back. "Great goal," she said.

"Yeah, that was great," Carrie said, coming up behind George. "You have such a strong kick."

"Thanks!" George said, smiling. "You were playing really tough, too."

Nancy smiled at George. Then she went over to find Melissa. Melissa was standing away from the other Tigers.

"Melissa," Nancy said. "I know you've been doing these things to the team. You put baby powder in the goalie's shirt, didn't you?"

Melissa looked away. Her face turned red. "How did you find out?" she asked.

"I remembered that your mom had a

baby," Nancy said. "Anyone could have baby powder, though. But then I saw you wearing those thick gloves."

Melissa looked down at her hands. She still had the red gloves on, but her hands looked thinner now.

"I think you put Amara's lucky gloves on under your own. That way you could sneak away with them and no one would see," Nancy said. "Am I right?"

Melissa nodded. "But please don't tell anyone," she pleaded with Nancy. "I don't want everyone to hate me. I just did it because I wanted a chance to play."

"Huh?" Nancy said. "I don't get it."

"My dad is really into soccer," Melissa said. "He used to be a soccer star in high school. He wants me to be a star, too. He yells a lot. I know he's disappointed when I don't get to play much."

"Yes," Nancy said. "He yells at everyone a lot."

"Well, I thought that if the really

good players couldn't play, then maybe Coach Santos would put me in instead. I want to play goalie. I'm really good at it when my dad and I practice."

"Did you ever tell Coach Santos that you wanted to play goalie?" Nancy asked.

"No," Melissa said, kicking the grass. "She'd probably just laugh since I'm no good at the other stuff. I can't run fast. But I'm good at blocking kicks. Really, I am."

"I believe you," Nancy said. "But you shouldn't have done all those mean things. Amara's shoe has been sticky ever since you put jelly in it. She hates that."

"I know," Melissa said. She kicked the grass again.

"Maybe you should talk to your dad," Nancy said. "Tell him how it makes you feel when he yells like that."

Melissa nodded slowly. "Do you have to tell Coach Santos I was the one who played the tricks?"

"No," Nancy said. "I'm not going to tell on you. You should talk to the coach yourself."

Just then the referee blew the whistle. The second half was starting. Nancy wasn't playing in the beginning of the second half, but Melissa was. She had to hurry to get onto the field.

Nancy watched happily from the sidelines. The Tigers played really well together, especially Carrie and George. They passed the ball back and forth. The Lions scored three times, making it 3–1. But then, in the last few minutes, Carrie scored a goal. The final score was Lions 3–Tigers 2.

"We almost beat the Lions!" Carrie announced happily, skipping off the field.

"But they're your best friends," George said. "Did you really want to beat them?"

"Of course," Carrie said. "I'm on the Tigers team now."

George gave Nancy a small smile as

Carrie walked away to change her shoes.

"Carrie's okay," George said when Carrie was gone.

"I think she was just trying to be friends with us," Nancy said. "And she didn't know how. That's why she was so pushy. She was trying to show us that she knew a lot about soccer so we'd like her."

George looked down at her feet. "I guess you're right," George said. "I feel bad. We didn't give her much of a chance."

"I know," Nancy said. "But maybe we can make up for it now."

"At the pizza party?" George asked.

"The pizza party!" Nancy said. "I almost forgot!"

Coach Santos was taking the whole team out for pizza. They were celebrating the end of the season.

"Great!" Nancy said. "Let's ask Carrie to sit with us."

George nodded. Then she and Nancy

walked over to their backpacks and sat down on the ground.

A minute later Melissa and her father walked by. Mr. Adams had his hand on Melissa's shoulder.

"I brought a plastic bag full of salt to the game, too," Melissa was saying. "I pretended to get a drink of water, and I put the salt in the cooler. I put jelly in Amara's shoe, and I let the air out of Julia's soccer ball."

"I'm sorry," said Melissa's father. "I shouldn't have yelled so much. I'm proud of how you played today. Winning isn't everything, Melissa. I just want you to have fun."

Melissa looked up at her father. "I had to sneak around a lot. I didn't like what I did."

Her father nodded. He leaned over and hugged Melissa.

"Will you help me tell Coach Santos about what I did?" Melissa asked.

"Yes," Mr. Adams said. "We'll go talk to her right now."

He held out his hand. Melissa put her

hand in her father's hand. The two of them began to walk across the soccer field toward Coach Santos.

Just then Lindsay Mitchell came over and joined them.

"I just heard Melissa say she had something important to tell her father," said Lindsay. "But I couldn't hear what it was."

George and Nancy giggled. Lindsay was such a gossip.

"Did you hear what she said?" asked Lindsay.

"Her father told Melissa that he was proud of the way she played today," said Nancy.

"Oh," said Lindsay. She sounded disappointed.

George stood up. "I'm hungry!" she said.

"Me, too," said Lindsay.

"I'm hungry, too," Nancy said. "But there's only one problem."

"What?" George asked.

"I can't find my shoes," Nancy said.

"Not again!" George cried.

George looked around on the grass. She looked under all the backpacks, especially her own. But Nancy's shoes weren't anywhere.

"Hey," Nancy said to George. "Your backpack is bulging. Let me see it."

Nancy opened George's backpack— and found her sneakers inside.

"No!" George shouted, laughing. "I didn't do it! I'm not the shoe thief again!"

"Yes, you are," Nancy said. "But not really. I just remembered. I didn't have room in my backpack this morning. So I stuffed my sneakers in your backpack."

It took Nancy only a minute to change into her sneakers. Then it was time to go get pizza with her friends. All of them! Even her newest friend— Carrie Rodis.

But first Nancy took out her notebook and opened it to the most recent page. At the bottom of the page she wrote:

Today I solved the soccer mystery and learned something about the game.

I found out that it doesn't matter what the score is—there's only one good way to win. Be a real friend to everyone on your team!

Case closed.